Creel3

Selected by

Matthew de Abaitua, Dr James Canton, Dr Holly Pester

Edited by

Danielle Bell, Lelia Ferro, Molly Shrimpton, Marieke Sjerps

With an introduction by

Dr Adrian May

University of Essex: Centre for Creative Writing

www.wivenhoebooks.com

Contents

i	Foreword - *Dr Adrian May*
1	At Halstatt - *Elaine Ewart*
2	Migrating Snipe: Brussels, April 2013 - *Elaine Ewart*
3	Absence - *Elaine Ewart*
4	Mehalah - *Lelia Ferro*
5	The Witch of Wivenhoe - *Lelia Ferro*
6	LiVING dIVISiON - *Steph Driver*
7	Gunpowder, Slate Mines and Salt - *Ruth Bradshaw*
12	Stone Gift - *Judith Wolton*
13	Fishing in the Highlands - *Judith Wolton*
14	Elements of Childhood - *Barbara Claridge*
17	Bench - Frinton Beach - *Melissa Shales*
18	Bench - Eastgate - *Melissa Shales*
19	The Charity Shop Wars - *Emma Kittle*
24	Marie Curie - *Marieke Sjerps*
26	Questions - *Jonathan King*
28	The Jar of Sibyl - *Wendy Constance*
33	Essex Vice - *Simon Everett*
34	Banks - *Simon Everett*
35	A Relationship with Rock - *Molly Shrimpton*
38	About the Contributors
40	About the Editors
41	Acknowledgements

Foreword

The teacher learns from the student, so the cliché, or truism goes. But this idea does have some sense in it, as, contrary to popular education as information-dump in preparation for employability orthodoxies, education, especially in the creative arts, is far more of exchange, a continuum, a tradition, even. I believe that whatever else we do, we create a culture of creativity, which is more of a mutual way of being than a measurable learning 'outcome'.

Creative students will challenge, vary, improvise on what they learn and make it new, while somehow keeping the old song of the human condition sung. We want bravery and hope from new writers, who seem recently to have got this, via a new positive view of the political.

Creel has been a place where this energy is displayed, where the work has its own urgency to take writing seriously, to be part of a community of creativity, with a wide but inclusive amount of experimentation and professionalism.

So it goes almost without saying that I'm proud of these writers who are part of our creative world, here in Essex, where courage still counts.

Dr Adrian May
Deputy Director of Creative Writing
Department of Literature, Film, and Theatre Studies
University of Essex

Creel3

Elaine Ewart
At Hallstatt

We thought it was a mistake, a joke,
when we got off the train at the edge of a lake
with no road or path. No sound except a hum,
a speck on the horizon, growing. As though in a dream,
we saw a boat arriving, unsummoned, to fetch us.
In the mirrored water, the splash of surf broke up
the glassy green and blue-white of mountain and sky.
The boatman was silent.

We docked at a settlement crouched on the shore;
a village of locked doors. Breathing hopeful clouds,
clapping our brittle hands to warm them,
we rang our blunt, echoing boots on the stone steps
up to the chapel. In the cemetery, fresh flowers
burnt orange and brown on the graves
while candles flamed behind red glass.

We came face to face with the charnel house;
stacks of skulls grinning back at us, powerless
against the comic: *Alas, poor gottle of gear.*
Their temples were painted with garlands;
some had their names in black gothic script,
tender and individual.

They told us nothing of wisdom: no more
than the rattle of bone in a box.
I wondered if laughter, now, would
set off an avalanche.

Migrating Snipe: Brussels, April 2013

Once, the night had a deep-sea denseness
that wrapped them about, those waders,
as their arrowed wings pointed them

to the sleeping city. As they flew, the stars above
wheeled in their heads. Not long ago,
even here, under jaundiced clouds,

we lay in our apartment blocks, innocent
of the wisp of snipe that twice a year
passed outside our open windows.

Every so often, a moorland chirrup
would puncture our fume-filled dreams.
Without waking, we would turn

and roll the blanket-scape around us.
But now, on the cathedral tower,
is a new, floodlit nest of predators.

As the snipe skirt crenellations,
the electric glare, beating down,
is yellow as the eye of the stooping falcon.

Plucked and picked over, the kill is carried
to the peregrine young, at the feet
of the stone-faced apostles of light.

Absence

The world rushed in to fill the gap you left;
A lap and flood, knocking against stones,
Echoes underwater, like whales calling.

Lelia Ferro
Mehalah

On the bed of the Blackwater,
a deadly embrace loosens,
fish rip away fleshy slivers,
bones reveal themselves.

Ebb drains the silver veins,
leaving a skull in the silt,
wrapped in raven hair,
sockets veiled in bladderwrack.

The haws clawing to the Ray,
drip berry blood into the river,
as spellbound crows step-dance,
to conjure a fire-eyed hare.

She zigzags across the saltings,
a silhouette on the gold sky,
grazing on purple asters,
resting on moonlit tombstones.

The Witch of Wivenhoe

It wasn't the done thing
to walk in woods at dusk,
acorn cracks beneath boots,
hair dangled in the water.

She didn't want to share
the velvet owl howls,
the blue moonlit lichen,
her throne up in the oak.

In the silver river -
her reflection slowly alters,
tonight she is a seal,
listening to mud pop.

On the day she vanished,
the crows danced on the oak,
below a starlit sky,
reflected on the water.

Living dIVISiON

BY STePH

Iodine

I
Iodine

I B Ir Th
Iodine Boron Iridium Thorium

I Ga I N SeN Se
Iodine Gallium Iodine Nitrogen Selenium Nitrogen Selenium

I F I Ti N He Re
Iodine Fluorine Iodine Titanium Nitrogen Helium Rhenium

I F Al Te Ra Nd F Al Lu Nd Er
Iodine Fluorine Aluminium Tellurium Radium Neodymium Fluorine Aluminium Lutetium Neodymium Erbium

Y O U Ce As Eu Nd Er S Ta Nd I N Ga N Y N O I Se
Yttrium Oxygen Uranium Cerium Arsenic Europium Neodymium Erbium Sulphur Tantalum Neodymium Iodine Nitrogen Gallium Nitrogen Yttrium Nitrogen Oxygen Iodine Selenium

Y O U Re B U F Fm Y As S I S Ta Nce
Yttrium Oxygen Uranium Rhenium Boron Uranium Fluorine Fermium Yttrium Arsenic Sulphur Iodine Sulphur Tantalum Nitrogen Cerium

Y O U C Ru S H O Th Er N Es S
Yttrium Oxygen Uranium Carbon Ruthenium Sulphur Hydrogen Oxygen Thorium Erbium Nitrogen Einsteinium Sulphur

Y O U P Ar Ti Ti O N
Yttrium Oxygen Uranium Phosphorus Argon Titanium Titanium Oxygen Nitrogen

Y
Yttrium

Yttrium

Oxygen

Uranium

Ruth Bradshaw
Gunpowder, Slate Mines and Salt

Late on the morning of Christmas Eve, I leave my parents' house in Penrhyndeudraeth and walk down out of the village. I want to clear my head of the long, dark drive north and west the night before. The mountains of Snowdonia beckon, but I only have an hour to spare so can't stray too far.

I walk towards the bridge over the Dywyrd Estuary. To my left is an area of industrial units. I concentrate on the view in the other direction, over the railway line and beyond it, to the sheep-dotted saltmarsh stretching out to the sea. A notice tied to the fence further along advertises salt lamb for sale at the local butcher. I pass the footpath which leads out over a level crossing and under the buzzing, fizzing power lines. This takes you to a house so far out on the marsh that it is one of the few places around here where the view of the estuary is free of the road and railway and pylons, which line this stretch of coast. It's a wonderful view, but one that must rarely be appreciated from inside the house. Whenever I have walked out that way, I've found the house empty and all the windows shuttered, perhaps as protection against the weather as much as to deter intruders.

Today I turn away from the sea, but I am still heading to a place where salt has shaped the environment. After passing through a gate behind the industrial units, I arrive in a very different landscape. Here the low-lying, flat lands of the estuary give way to steep-sided narrow valleys filled with birch and oak trees, where even on this mid-winter day the air is filled with the sound of birdsong and gently running water. Not so long ago this was a very different place, for this was once the biggest explosive works in Europe, where a combination of ammonium nitrate, glycerine and salt was used to make gunpowder. For 130 years from 1865 on, hundreds of people were employed here, and the products they made had an impact on the lives of millions more. But for the past two decades, Gwaith Powdwr (The Powder Works) has been a nature reserve, a peaceful place where bats roost and nightjars breed.

The industry more commonly associated with Snowdonia is slate mining, but even though the production at Gwaith Powdwr was chemical rather than mineral, this is another place where human history is completely bound up with its geology. The three parallel valleys made the site ideal for manufacturing gunpowder; splitting production between them limited the impact of any accidental explosions. But it was never completely safe. Employees were killed here as recently as the 1980s, and the products they made were used to deadly effect elsewhere. Business boomed during the global conflicts of the twentieth century – 17 million grenades were filled here during World War Two – and the works also supplied explosives to the mining industry.

Trees and plants now fill the spaces where once so many earned their living making deadly devices. Most of the buildings, pipelines and conveyors, which were needed to manufacture the explosives, were removed during decommissioning in the 1990s. Many of the remaining structures are only visible as ghostly remnants, half-hidden among the woods and scrub, but a few have been preserved intact. I follow a track up through the site to the place where the explosives shed still stands. This has an inner building surrounded by a separate outer wall, several feet thick and made of sand bags, which is intended to force any accidental explosion upwards rather than outwards. This wall is now a patchwork of vibrant greens and mottled browns, as ferns and other plant life gradually colonise the sand bags.

Leaving the woodland, I emerge into a more open grassy area and get my first views out of the site and over to the mountains of Snowdonia. This is all the incentive I need to continue to the top of the furthest valley, where another of the remaining buildings stands. The pendulum shed is where the strength of gunpowder was tested. Workers fired it from a cannon into a huge metal pendulum and measured the resulting movement. Once, local people could set their clocks by the daily boom of this gunpowder test, but now the explosives and cannon are long gone and only the pendulum remains. This is my favourite part of the site; from here there is a panoramic view of the National Park, which this place is not quite a part of. The park boundary skirts inland for a few miles around Penrhyndeudraeth, as the area around Gwaith Powdwr was excluded when Snowdonia National Park was created in the 1950s.

I close my eyes and try to imagine what this place would have been like in the middle of the last century when it was a busy industrial site. I can hear the clank and rattle of the conveyor belts moving materials around the site, and the revving of engines and beeping of horns as trucks arrive and depart to transport the explosives to coal mines across the country. Most of the human voices are drowned out by the machinery, but occasionally I hear a shout as one of the workers calls out. I try to picture those workers too, the men and women who travelled from miles around to do this dirty, dangerous, noisy work.

Now, all that is gone and I have the site to myself. I've only rarely seen other people here in all the times I've visited, and I have never encountered anybody else walking out here from the village. Perhaps if you live so close to the sea and the mountains, it's enough to know they are there.

Looking out at the view from the pendulum shed on Christmas Day two years ago, I saw a rainbow. Today there is neither rain nor sun but surprisingly good visibility for such a murky day. In one direction, I can see out over the glistening saltmarsh and the widening estuary to the sea. Harlech Castle is just visible as a dark grey smudge against the paler grey sky to the south, and to the north a glimpse of white reveals the village of Portmeirion. In the middle of the estuary is Ynys Giftan, less than a mile from the shore and accessible only at low tide. I walked out there one summer a few years back, at first trying to leap over each of the silvery channels which the sea has carved through the sand, but soon finding it easier to discard my boots and paddle through the sun-warmed water instead. Ynys Giftan is uninhabited now, but for much of the twentieth century it was home to a farming family. Their ruined farmhouse remains, gradually disappearing into the scrub that now covers most of the island. If there was treasure on this island, I didn't find it. Instead I picnicked on the beach and enjoyed a new perspective on the familiar view out to sea.

Today, the view from the pendulum shed prompts other memories too – of sunny days on the beach at Harlech, and of walking in all kinds of weather in the mountains that surround me. To the south, I can just make out the start of the Rhiongydd, the wilder, less visited mountains that I have come to know and love in the last few years; to the north are the rounded humps of Moel Hebog on one side and the Moelwynion on the other. I've climbed Moelwyn Mawr and its distinctive Matterhorn-shaped neighbour Cnicht more times than I can remember. I've known these mountains since my childhood, when we spent many holidays in the slate-tipped "hole" in the middle of the National Park, the area of slate quarries around Blaenau Ffestiniog that was also excluded when they drew the Park boundary.

It seems ironic now that such care went into ensuring the National Park was untouched by industry and then just a few years later, construction began on Trawsfynydd Nuclear Power Station. Now that too is redundant and slowly being decommissioned, but for the time being, its bulky form remains, looking like a bloated, deformed castle from a distance. Meanwhile the slate tips are a visible legacy of the area's proud industrial heritage, and as much a part of the landscape as the sheep-grazed mountains that surround them.

When I was a small child, my parents owned a half-share in a house in Dolrhedyn just below the slate tips, and so close to a stream that the sound of the rushing water would lull us to sleep at night. 'Bye bye slate, bye bye stream, bye bye sheep,' we would chant as we drove back over the Crimea Pass at the end of another summer weekend spent swimming in the stream and building dens in the bracken. It rains a lot here, even more than in other parts of Wales, so there must also have been long, dull days spent stuck inside while the rain teemed down outside, but I have fewer memories of these.

As one by one, my siblings and I became teenagers and our parents finally succumbed to our pleas for holidays abroad, we came less often, but for years we spent at least part of every school holiday and many weekends here. Most of those visits included at least one walk up the track between the stream and the slate tips to the Cwmorthin valley. As our legs grew longer these walks would continue up the inclines built to serve the mines, and then on to the summits of nearby mountains. When we were younger, we often didn't get any further than Cwmorthin.

Here we explored the ruins of the terraced houses that were once inhabited by the quarrymen and their families. Everything in these houses – the walls, the floors, the roofs, the doorsteps and windowsills, even the fences separating one small garden from the next – was constructed from the same grey slate. Now those slates are gradually collapsing back onto the ground from which they were dug. We would scramble about among the piles of fallen stones, searching unsuccessfully for possessions abandoned by the former residents and pretending to cook on the empty hearths. Some of these houses were still occupied as recently as the 1940s, within my parents' lifetimes, but as a small child that seemed such an impossibly long time ago that they may as well have been the remains of pre-historic dwellings.

At the time, I gave little thought to the people who lived in this remote and inaccessible place - a mile or more's walk to the nearest paved road at Dolrhedyn, and even further to a shop or a pub. Now I know more about the dangers and diseases the quarrymen faced; about the unhealthy, overcrowded living conditions and the risks from rock falls and slate dust. So, I find myself thinking about their lives, and particularly of the women who tried to make homes in these damp dwellings. How did they feel as they waved their children off on the long walk down the mountain to school each day? Or as they waited for the men to return from their dangerous work in the mine? Even if they had time to stop and admire the beauty of the surrounding landscape, did that provide much compensation for all the worrying and hardship?

I wonder what the former residents of those houses would have made of the brightly clad walkers and climbers who now pass here on their way up Cnicht. Would they be puzzled by all the people who choose to spend their leisure time walking the same tracks along which the quarrymen trudged to and from work each day? Or think it strange that people pay to visit slate mines? And stranger still that some pay even more to bounce their way round abandoned slate caverns on a trail of trampolines, or hurl themselves down steep hillsides on specially constructed mountain bike trails? Adventure tourism and outdoor recreation has replaced mining as the local industry here, and these hills, where once so many lived and too many died, have become a playground.

I make another short visit to Gwaith Powdwr on the afternoon of Boxing Day. I'm with my mum this time and the daylight is already fading when we arrive. It is the promise of a beautiful sunset that has drawn us here so late in the day. I slow my pace to match mum's. The pendulum shed is out of reach today. Instead we stop at a bench about two thirds of the way up the valley nearest the estuary, next to a sign which commemorates the site's former life, and I think of how people and places change. Who now would be willing to accept the kind of conditions that the miners worked in? Or to live in somewhere as inaccessible as Cwmorthin or Ynys Giftan? The slate mines and Gwaith Powdwr have changed so much, but some things stay the same. We sit and look out over the saltmarsh and the sea, and watch the huge golden sun disappear quickly out of sight.

Judith Wolton

Stone Gift

You gave me a stone from Aldeburgh beach.
It lies in the palm of my hand,
rests on my lifeline.
Smooth and grey, it does not hurt,
it is light enough to carry.
My hand curls round it, holds it safe
like a talisman.

It stores in its soul flint
and ice, millions of years
of rolling among shingle.
It knows the taste of salt, the crash of waves,
the cold battering of a shifting shoreline.

Yet in my hand it is warm, almost soft,
strong in its smoothness.
Its hardened heart sits deep inside
telling old stories.

Fishing in the Highlands

When the highlands were deserts
you were there,
following rivers,
swimming in lakes.

You were there as waters dried,
rivers shrank
and lakes stagnated.
some of you died, drifted

and sank. Rubble washed down,
crushed your bones,
flattened your flesh,
left you petrified.

Spiny fish, armoured fish
stencilled in Old Red Sandstone,
strata fine as millefeuille,
glass eyes blind.

You slept folded in Devonian beds
raised from under the sea
to the high glens.
Now we disturb

your rest and slice you,
lay you out in light again -
such delicate lace
cased in plate glass.

Barbara Claridge
Elements of Childhood

Catherine liked high places
High up on the hills

She dreamt of children's voices
A woman of the hills

The words from a PJ Harvey folk song, *The Wind,* refer to Saint Catherine's Chapel, which stands on a limestone hill above the village of Abbotsbury on the Dorset coast. It is a place where children should go. As the chapel was built in the late 14th Century on a Benedictine Monks' pilgrimage route, today's children would have to shout for Saint Catherine to hear, and they usually do. If you are accompanying thirty children you must factor in teaching and child-watching as well as seeking the spirit in a place for yourself.

From the village main street, turn left through a rough wooden gate to join the path leading to the chapel at the top of the hill. The gate always causes some amusement to town children who must wait in turn patiently and then pretend to be disgusted when the teachers call out, 'Kissing gate.'
  'Always remember to say hello to the man with the dog,' because there is usually a man with a dog.
  In the open field most children prefer to stay close when they see real cows and some begin the climb on their own but give up to wait, puffing and blowing. Given the freedom to decide, a few sprint all the way to the top effortlessly. 'What kept you?' they say when the teachers arrive.

Only make a visit on a clear day when the water in the sea is shining; choose carefully your pilgrimage. In high places children and teachers can dream of their future. Only go when the grass is moderately dry and take time to lie on your back and look at the sky. No one can move for three minutes. (We couldn't be still for more.) 'What do you see? What are the clouds saying?' When all the breath is returned and the breathing is easy (for it is a steep climb) we sit up and the lesson begins.

From this height, we can see a community. To the north-east a ribbon of development swings like a hammock from side to side across the valley floor, which dips gradually to the sea. Buildings appear like Toytown; the church, the houses and the tithe barn. We discuss the building materials – a local quarried limestone called golden bluff and the style and pitch of the rooves; the small windows and doors. 'If you could build this village what would you add?'

'Let's walk around St. Catherine's.'

We prepare to look the other way towards the sea. This involves picking everything up from our temporary camp, bags, books, coats and all, to walk to the top of the hill and past the chapel door. From the ridge, looking down to the south, we can see all spread before us as if we are on top of the highest mountain: the Fleet lagoon, the shore, the sea, Portland, Chesil, the Swannery. Every time, children show similar reactions; predictable and, at the same time, reassuring. From the observation point the teacher has a living presentation and real visual aids for outdoor geography, a lesson that children will remember all their lives. It is easy to explain the geographical features, to teach about salinity in seawater and show the lagoon bound by the spit of Chesil Bank; how it protects the landward side and makes a sanctuary for the swans; how the hard stone of Portland resists the erosion of the waves and makes a tied island; how the chapel was a prominent landmark to seafarers. It is so good for us to be outside and learning.

The children, calmer after listening, sit down and take their time; they draw a sketch or a map, then write a poem; always a poem. But their vocabulary is appropriately technical and comes easily to them now. 'Remember to ask a question and include something about your feelings.' Sally writes for Ben because he can think and she can write.

We tiptoe into the church and learn about triple windows in the east wall and why the easterly direction of this window in a church is important. We look at the stone-roof vaulting and wonder who could have carried those heavy stones, and St Catherine smiles at the now hushed voices of the children.

Within a very short time we are all scrunching, slipping and tripping over the shingle ridges of Chesil Beach. This one landmark is stitched into the geography of my own school days, when it was necessary to memorise real examples without ever visiting them. Spit: Chesil Beach and Orford Ness. Chalk cliffs: Dover and the Seven Sisters, Seaford, Sussex. Pyramidical peak: the Matterhorn. Strange facts to remember for so long without a context.

So here, a textbook example comes to life at last. This beach or shingle bank is eighteen miles long and stretches from West Bay to Portland. A depositional landform, fairly stable for at least five thousand years. The seaward side shelves steeply to the sea in a series of ridges running parallel to the water, and the slope continues well below water level where tidal backwash can drag you under. This is a place for careful teaching.

We sit in groups at the top of the ridge and discuss the pebbles above the noisy swash. 'This is what you do: you have ten minutes to look very carefully around you and select ten pebbles. Then with a partner show your collection and explain what you like about each stone and why you picked it. What does it remind you of? Listen to your partner. Ask questions.' Totally absorbed children fix their eyes on the stones, sorting colours and shapes and sifting noisy flints between their fingers. The teacher calls when ten minutes are up. 'Now… put nine pebbles back exactly where you found them and keep only one. Write why you kept this very one…'

Chesil is a barrier beach, although in the past some experts have classified it as a tombolo (from the word tumulus: mound), a depositional landform where an island, in this case Portland, is tied to the mainland by a spit or a bar. The unusual feature of Chesil is that the ridges are parallel rather than perpendicular to the shoreline. The geography is almost beyond primary age comprehension, but I explain about diagenesis and silicification to Harry who hates writing anything but knows more than me.

As we walk back and away from the beach we think about eighteen miles and eighteen billion pebbles, graded carefully by the sea from peas in the west, to oranges in the east. It is said that smugglers, landing on the beach in pitch-black-no-star-nights, could tell exactly where they were by the size of the pebbles. Children like that story.

Melissa Shales
Bench – Frinton Beach

Sky sailing
Pirouetting
Sails flapping
Wind whirling
Waves roaring
Foam surging
Dog yapping
Child shouting
Man laughing
Scarf flying
Ears tingling
On the clifftop
Brass plaque
Fingers reading
She sits
Still
Listening
White cane resting
She has been benched

Bench – Eastgate

For approximately the 487th time
In the roughly 4383 minutes
I've had to wait
At the bus stop
Halfway
Between my front door and the railway crossing gate
I wish
For a bench
Average waiting time nine minutes
When I win the postcode lottery
I will buy a bench
To sit and watch the traffic jam
It will have graffiti
That will make old women laugh
And shock the young

Emma Kittle

The Charity Shop Wars

I'd made the journey all the way from London to the estuary town of Collingtree, but after eventually finding parking on one of the steep, narrow roads leading from the high street, I knock at my Aunt Jean's bungalow door to find she isn't in. No sign of the dogs either. I have to admit I'm a bit disappointed. On the way here I had the good idea that she might try to help out her favourite nephew with a bit of cash, just to tide me over of course, like she used to.

I thought I'd hang around just for a bit to see if she'd come back, she might just be walking the dogs or something. But the grey sky I followed here finally cracks and I duck into what I thought was a hardware store. Turns out it's a Pet Rescue charity shop, a kind of pop-up charity shop. The two ladies at the counter stare at me for a moment before one of them turns her attention back to a girl looking through some junk.

'Are you slim under there, love? Skinny? Gorgeous slip over here. Sexy. Suit a lovely young thing like you.' The object of their attention is a girl in a purple hat and a large overcoat, who turns and flares her nostrils at me.

'What is it you're after, love?' One of the ladies is right next to her, and I begin to pretend to look through the books.

'A round knitting needle,' she says.

'Oh where have I seen one? I know I've seen one somewhere. I know. I have one at home,' says the shop assistant. 'Are you local?'

'I work at the health food store, I've just started,' says the girl in the hat.

'I'll get it for you, bring it, bring it to the shop if you like. I'll do it tomorrow.'

'That's very kind of you,' says the girl. I have a peek over and I see her delicate pink cheek.

'Yes, I'll find it tonight and bring it to you tomorrow. What was your name?'

'Sarah.'

'I'll do that for you then, Sarah.' The woman goes back to her place behind the glass counter and the two ladies serving at the Pet Rescue charity shop counter continue to chat.

I start to wander around. The place is a mess, and full of junk. Cheap creased shoes and small ceramic earthenware from the mid-90s. I can smell that gurchy musty smell and a waft of something acrid rising from the warming damp of my coat.

The first voice is loud again. 'That pompous Miranda,' she says. 'Always feel like she's looking down on me, know what I mean, Brenda?'

'That's what she's like, isn't it?'

'Don't know how she got like that, do you?'

'Don't know how any of us get the way we are. We just do, don't we?'

The rain on the crowded window is cocooning us in, a water curtain steaming up at the edges. It's warm in here. Maybe too warm. I stop in front of a gold cabinet and look at a basket of odds and ends, listening to the women, aware of the girl. I let out a little laugh when I pick up a round stone and wonder if she notices. But then, on the flat side, underneath, I see that it is not just a stone but a fossil. I hold it in my palm carefully so it cannot be seen by them and look at the imprint. It's an imprint of a fish. A fish with feet.

Now I know that in the shop I pass every day on the Kensington Church Street, the one on my way back from work, beautiful fossils go for an arm and a leg. I walk home slowly, looking in the windows, dragging the time before I get back. And now I feel a small tremor in my belly.

'What you got, love?' Brenda is standing right beside me.

'I was just thinking that my son would love this to add to his collection of stones.'

'Ooh, yes, I'm sure,' she says. 'Haven't you got a game about telling the time behind there Jill? She's got a game about telling the time behind there, I bet he would like that too.'

'Yes, I'm sure,' I say.

Jill sighs and drops down from her stool. 'It'll be a great game for learning to tell the time,' she says, 'the little boy will love it. What's his name?'

'Um. Sebastian.'

'Here it is.' Jill lifts a plastic board game onto the counter. Some of the numbers are missing. 'I think they're in the box. That's a lovely one for your kid.'

'Yes, I'm sure he would love it. So how much is it?'

'£1?'

'And for the rock?' '

'£1.50 altogether.'

I search through my pockets and can't find anything now. Not even a penny. Nothing in my wallet either. 'Can you hold them for me while I go and get some cash?'

'As long as you come back,' Jill says. 'I mean the clock game won't hang around forever. I bet someone would love that clock game. You got any kids, love?'

'No,' says the purple-hatted girl, still looking at the knitting needles.

'Don't you worry,' I say, flashing them a wide grin. 'I'm an honest man, I'll be back in a jiff.' The bell rattles as I open the door and run through the rain to the cash point over the road. Rushing to type my pin, I get it wrong. I hear the bell tinkle, and I flick my eyes towards the shop door which is just closing. The cash point is beeping at me. Do I want a receipt yes or no? YES, I mean, NO.

'Here's the honest gentleman,' Brenda sighs. 'Your purchases are all wrapped up for you, sir.'

Jill hands over a creased and yellowed Morrison's bag with the plastic clock game and a package wrapped in newspaper inside. 'We don't have no change for a tenner. Don't get many customers buying things with notes in here,' she shouts.

They both look at me and I say, 'Well, you'd better keep the change, ladies.'

'Are you sure? That's VERY kind of you. That's very kind isn't it, Jill? He's honest AND kind.'

'Don't get many like that, do you?' Jill booms as I hold the bag away from my coat cuff.

'Not at all. And can I just say that you ladies are doing a great job here, at the…' I search for an indication of the charity's name, 'Pet Rescue.'

Holding my prize carefully and yet consciously I wonder what other treasures I might find in this small town. Wonder what it's worth? Even just within my view are two other charity shops on this very same street.

The second charity shop is a pile of crap too. But I'm careful to scan the place, the worn clothes, the kids' stuff for a pound, the bric-a-brac.

I cross the road and am thinking about getting back to Jean's when I see the other one, which looks more like a ladies' clothes shop, but as I look closely I can see a few royal wedding mugs. It's another charity shop – Melth. As I enter, they're hoovering. 'Oh pardon me,' I say, 'are you closing?'

'Ooh no,' says the bobbed elderly lady, 'just trying to fit it in between customers!'

'Ah good.' I wander around, appreciating the spacious, well managed racks of clothes. A nice zigzagged scarf in the men's section I see is £15. £15. And it looks worn around the edges. But still, the shop's more pleasant to peruse: bigger, airier, spacious and neat. In the bric-a-brac section one of the ladies is on her knees, moving things around. I hear her sniff gently before she moves out of my way. I hear her whisper, 'That's all done Miranda.' I scan the shelves above where she was dusting. On a little wire stand, could have been made especially for it, is a fossil just like the one I have in the bag.

As I stare at it I feel none of the earlier excitement. What a fool, I say to myself. A tenner for that old stone. When really they're ten a penny. What a goddam fool. Jean never knew that about me, did she? Can't get anything right. So I leave the shop, still conscious of the dirty wrinkled carrier bag in my hand.

The sky is darkening as I head back toward the street where the car is parked. The rain's stopped but I'm shivering. Forget Jean and her dogs. I get in and fling the bag onto the seat. As I pass the estuary the swans are still strutting about. I push down the window and cast it out towards them, hoping I might hit one. I put down my foot and get the hell out of there.

As I work at my desk, getting the figures to balance for the taxman, I turn to see the close up of the fossil on the muted TV screen. I grab the controller and switch on the sound. The stone fish darts away and there is a local news reporter talking to a young girl with pink cheeks. 'So you say you found it here? In a charity shop?'

'Yes, at the Melth shop. Over there. I showed it to my boss and he said that he knew of a pair of fish fossils a local woman had once owned that were said to be really important, but she hid them away and no-one ever knew if the story was true. So it made me wonder if this could be one, and I took it to an old chap at Fulton. Knows everything about the teeth and remains found around here.' The news cuts amateurishly, in my view, to a red tower and a windy cliff.

'And here he is,' says the newscaster, hair flipping over her eyes. A man with a white beard and an army hat stands bewildered, staring at the camera.

'So what can you tell us about the Collingtree fish fossils?' she asks.

'I been doing this job for fifty years and I discovered 53 million year old sharks' teeth but I never seen anything as ancient as this. It's the walking fish. Probably 375 million years old! For hundreds of years people have told the story of the east coast walking fish. A local myth. And here's the evidence to back up the stories.'

'And are you aware of the value of these stones to evolutionary scientists?'

Pause. 'I just said, didn't I?'

Pause. 'And you mentioned that from your knowledge of fish life you would say that this was a male specimen?'

'Yes. We're thrilled about this. Look carefully at the pockets around the bottom here, we think you can see the male reproductive organ, known as the clasper.'

'I see it there yes.' Pause. 'But, more to the point, what does it mean for the mental health charity, Melth? And the value of this fossil?'

'Well… the fossil's priceless,' he smiles. 'The only thing more valuable to us would be having a fossil of the female fish, given that we'd then have a pair. As far as a monetary value is concerned let's just say, the charity and the girl who's sharing it with them are very lucky.'

'And there you have it. A giant story in a small town, a very kind young girl, and a lot of money for the mental health charity, Melth. I don't think you could have a better story than that, but I wonder if Bill can beat it with his weather news?'

I think back to the moment when I opened the car window, the yellow bag and the waft of stale cigarette disappearing after it as I flung it out towards the river. My heart has sunk into my stomach but a little bit of my brain says, it might still be there. There's something else though. I'm not sure what it is. A flickering image of Brenda and the smelly Pet Rescue charity shop. There's something uncomfortable happening. My heart's flickering along with the images – Jean and her dirty windows, Brenda and the Pet Rescue shop. An honest gentleman. Maybe they could do with a bit of luck too.

Information on the accompanying image:
Photographer unknown, "Portrait of Marie Curie and her daughter Irene," (1925).
Rights: Wellcome Library, London. Copyrighted work available under Creative Commons. Attribution only licence CC BY 4.0.

Marieke Sjerps
Marie Curie

Her notes are waiting.
   She died for art.
   Now her art wants you to do the same.
   Navy blue scribblings, diagrams, cursive French. It's all waiting for you.
   You love libraries, so why don't you go? Find the Bibliothèque Nationale de France. Sign that liability waiver. Sign over your bag. Step into the protective gear. Step into the room. Now strip. You don't need protection. Run your bare fingers over the pages. They're happy you're here.
   It doesn't even have to be now. That radiation will last a thousand years and more. It killed the first woman to win a Nobel prize, so it can definitely take you. Little vials in her pockets, gently glowing. She called them fairy lights. Will-o'-the-wisps, they wait patiently.
   She's waiting too. The first woman to earn her tomb in the Panthéon lies in a lead-lined coffin. She radiates. Isn't that comforting? Marie wasn't scared. Dying and nearly blinded by cataracts, she didn't think the fairies had killed her. Imagine her in the sanatorium, seeing no danger. Her work had saved lives, how could it take hers?
   Her daughter Irène died of leukaemia. She chased the fairies too, bathed in their glow, won a Nobel Prize like her mother. She died. Look at this picture; mother and daughter at work together. Nine years and thirty-one, that's what they had left. Radiation lasts for millennia. So, Marie Curie's notes can wait. Her bones can wait. One day you'll dive into the archives. One day you'll find her in her leaden box. Maybe you'll win a golden medallion or two. Maybe your work will save millions. Maybe you'll take your life and transform it into art. You'll lie in your grave, not asleep; waiting, glowing.

Jonathan King
Questions

If the Jackdaw that struts across your lawn
like a soldier on parade
stopped and spoke to you of his loneliness,
would you listen?

If you could hear the cry of the salmon
caught in the eagle's claws,
would you care?

If you saw the fear in the eyes of the moth
trapped in the spider's web,
would you set it free?

Does the noise the doe makes
as she tries to find her way back
to the safety of the herd
disturb you?

When the leaf falls from the tree
do you feel sadness for its loss,
or joy at the change of seasons?

If you had just one wish
from a Djinn's lantern,
would you ask for your heart's desire?
Or would you set another free
from the prison of their own longing?

How many lies would it take
to awaken the phoenix of truth
that sleeps on your tongue?

and how many lives will you need to live
before you can look death in the face
and still walk the path you have chosen?

Have my questions
tightened the rope you bind yourself with,
or opened a door to a greater perception?

Only you have the answer.

I am just a white room
on a sunlit day,
with a mirror on every wall.
Wherever you turn
you will see your own reflection
looking back at you.

Will you live here?

Wendy Constance
The Jar of Sibyl

I thought it was happenstance. Imaginings of extreme disasters where the power of fire or water threatened planet Earth - swollen rivers surging down roads and cascading through houses; raging fires blazing through forests before skidding into towns; tsunami torrents smashing coastlines and wrecking structures of every scale; burnt-parched deserts creeping over fertile earth; fractured ice mountains crushing everything that crossed their landward course.

Manna for a writer seeking storylines to grab publishers' attention.

Dystopian fiction for Young Adults: I added humans - split them into two warring factions: the Fire Tribes, hungry and thirsty, trudging across barren burned lands of the interiors; and the Water Tribes, striving for survival against the tidal onslaught on the receding coastline fringes – each tribe wanting a slice of the other's lands and resources.

The books weren't best sellers, but my royalties were enough to pay the utility bills while my husband paid the mortgage. The nightmare visions happened randomly, some so frightening and real that I woke up riven with panic, had to reassure myself they hadn't really happened.

Which was alright until a news headline announced a disaster scarily similar to one of the nightmares.

And then another.

Was I foreseeing actual disasters before they happened?

No.

Just fluky coincidences.

They happen all the time, don't they?

I hadn't had any visions for a while when my own personal disaster struck - my husband wanted a divorce. (Why didn't I foresee that?) He moved his younger woman into the marital home and I moved in with Laura, my mother. After that my only nightmares were of a future stuck with Laura, who I knew felt the same.

Until the morning I awoke, gasping for breath, my head full of flickering images of fire engulfing the front of a train. I'd never *seen* anything so specific before, but that day Laura was going to meet her friend Marie in London using her Senior Rail Card (one of the few perks of getting older she said.)

And I knew it was the same train.

'You must get a later train,' I told Laura as she gazed in the mirror fluffing her hair.

'Why?' she asked, examining her neck for wrinkles that might reveal her age, before draping a soft green silk scarf round it.

'I've got a bad feeling about the train crashing.'

'Don't be ridiculous. Anyway, I can't because I'm booked on that train and it's not transferable.'

As Laura put on her coat my head heaved with noises: hysterical screeches clashing with moans of mangled metal. I grabbed hold of Laura, pleaded with her not to go.

'For goodness' sake Sibyl, you're making a fool of yourself,' she said with one last glance in the hall mirror to check her appearance.

I nearly let her go to meet her fate, for surely my vision was just that, there would be no train crash, but something primal coursed through me and I fell to my knees weeping by the front door.

What mother can leave her daughter, albeit a supposedly grown-up one, in such a wretched state? Not even mine it turned out. She cradled me in her arms, reawakening memories of early childhood. We hadn't hugged since I turned thirteen, which was when she decided I should start calling her Laura instead of Mum.

I let her soothe me; let her make me a cup of tea; let her talk of booking a doctor's appointment for me.

'I'll text Marie,' she said, 'Tell her I'll get the next train, though I'll have to pay extra!'

'I'm sorry,' I said, 'but you'll have to go another day. Even if you caught the next train it wouldn't get very far.'

'Why?'

'Because of the crash. The line will be blocked.'

'Ah, the crash,' she said, a whiff of sarcasm escaping, before doubt about my state of mind returned.

I heard her phone Marie, heard her whisper, 'I'm worried Sibyl is having a nervous breakdown. I don't think she's over the divorce.'

By this time I knew she'd missed the train, so I relaxed, but I needed fresh air. I could smell the burning that was still inside my head. Laura agreed to a walk, anything to pacify the daughter she thought was losing her marbles. We walked until I knew it had happened. When we reached home I turned on the television - flashing across the bottom of the screen - 'Update on horrific train crash.'

My yelp was part distress, part triumph (wrong I know.) Laura clasped her throat, whispering, 'Oh my god,' and it was my turn to make tea as I told her about all my visions; how they'd been the inspiration for my books.

'You've been given a gift,' said Laura, 'Some say a gift can be a curse, but not if you use it wisely. Make the most of it dahling.'

Suddenly I was dahling.

By wisely she meant financially wise. Dad's death had left her less well-off than she'd expected, which was the reason she'd agreed to my return - to help pay the household bills, so that she could still afford the beauty treatments she'd come to think of as necessities to fend off the ageing process.

Laura saw to it that my rise to fame as the Prophet Queen was as rapid as a wildfire in a drought-ravaged forest. It started with local newspaper and television interviews after she spread the word about my train crash warning. It shifted to national news when she "remembered" me telling her, years before my books were published, about the visions portending disasters which later happened.

'She was right wasn't she,' Laura beamed at the cameras, enjoying every second, especially the time spent in make-up. 'Her books prove it. You can check the dates.'

I became a celebrity, dubbed "The Prophet of Doom" by one newspaper - or "The Profit of Doom" as Laura called me. She lapped up the guest appearances on chat shows, not to mention helping me spend the huge advance on my new book deal as all my old books raced up the best-seller lists.

AP snaked into my life the following year, hailed as 'The King of Entertainment', a music mogul with top bands and singers under his wing, who insisted everybody called him by his initials. Nobody knew his real name.

He thought he would look good strutting about with the Prophet Queen, was indignant but persistent when I rejected his increasingly elaborate advances and offers of expensive gifts. The trouble with gods is that they expect to get what they want, so he offered what he thought was the ultimate experience - a trip to anywhere in the world on his private jet, AP0110, if I spent just one night with him.

'I don't do one night stands - even on luxury jets,' I said, with no intention of succumbing to a male lampooned by the press about his need to be treated like a god. 'I suppose you change the number after your initials after each woman, so you're hoping I'll be 0111.'

'Come on Sibyl,' he said 'Use your skills.'

'What do you mean?'

'You're a prophet, aren't you? Can't you see it?'

'I know what I can see – that you're not going to lure me onto that plane.'

'That plane - AP0110 - spells Apollo. That's me - god of music, truth and prophecy. That's why I want you, Sibyl. I've got the music, my musicians sing about truth, but I'm missing the prophecy.'

'No wonder you use initials if your parents chose to name you after a mythological Greek god.'

'Suppose I'm not a myth,' his eyes teasing as he spoke. 'Suppose I'm a real god. What wish would you have me grant in return for one night of making love on the Apollo?'

'Get lost.'

'Anything you like. Just say it, I'll arrange it.'

'Why would I do that?'

'Let's say to prove I am - or am not - a god.'

I'm not sure why my thoughts turned to Laura and her fears of dying and getting old, but to call AP's bluff, I asked to live forever.

'You got me,' he said. 'Gods can't grant immortality to mortals.'

'You said I could ask for whatever I want.'

'How about a long life? You name the number of years.'

'Okay,' I said, to shut him up. 'Give me a thousand years and I'll spend a night with you on the Apollo.'

'Deal,' he said.

'Funny, but I don't feel any different.'

'You will. You're a true prophetess, so you'll know, but remember that once granted it can't be changed.'

We parted and I avoided him for several months, deleted his messages asking, 'Seen anything yet?' It wasn't funny. I hadn't had any visions in that time, but the latest book was selling well, so there was no hurry to write another.

One morning I woke to a shimmering image of fireworks on a news bulletin, trumpeting the arrival of 2217.

It seemed so real, like the train crash, but couldn't be.

It was two hundred years away!

That day AP arrived at the studio where I was doing an interview, and started harassing me for a date for the "Apollo experience". I told him where to put his precious jet. Mustering his godly fury he said he'd done his part of the deal, he knew I'd had a vision to prove it, so I should do my part.

'There is no deal,' I said, ignoring his reference to a vision, 'You're no god, and I won't live to be a thousand.'

'Mortals!' he spat. 'Such fools, who fear getting old and dying, who think you can outwit the gods. You accepted the thousand years, Sibyl. You'll regret rejecting me.'

'I don't think so.'

'You didn't ask for eternal youth. By the time you're a thousand years old you'll be less than a withered husk, aching for death.'

Bastard god – why didn't I *see* he was Apollo reincarnated, and I was descended from the ancient Sibyls?

Centuries passed and I worked hard, peddling my prophecies to princesses, presidents and profiteers - to afford the latest age-defying potions and peels which advancing science created. At least I was able to treat Laura to a face-lift before she died with a permanent smile drawn tightly across her face.

But I couldn't stop *seeing* more droughts; more floods; more fires; more famines leading to devastated natural habitats, emaciated carcasses, mass extinctions. Horrors that scorched every one of my senses. A future where humans were increasingly intent on destroying themselves and the planet. The fireworks I'd *seen* to announce 2217 were in fact bomb blasts, the multi-colours displaying the different toxic compounds used. It was one way of reducing global population.

An unremitting resource for writing new stories about the Fire Tribes and the Water Tribes. Until there was nothing to write about and no way to write.

I became as ravaged as the land. The after-effects of chemical treatments, transplants, laser surgery, and grafts meant there was no skin left to treat, no body.

AP was right - not even a withered husk.

Laura had been right too - a gift can be a curse.

All that remained was my voice, vacuum-sealed in a jar.

At last 3017 arrived. I cried out, my pitch so high the jar shattered. I escaped with the shards, free to the elements, free at last to die.

Free to glimpse a future where, as I, the last mortal on this planet, expired, rain fell from the heavens, green shoots and tiny ants emerged from the parched earth.

The Cumaean Sibyl accepted the offer of 1,000 years life from Apollo in return for his love. When she rejected him he said she would not have eternal youth to match her long life. Her body withered into nothing but a voice, kept in a jar.

Simon Everett
Essex Vice

Late August vibe
Crockett's Theme by
Jan Hammer up the east
west axis Southend to Leigh
could've been the 80s
synth riff
goldenrod chinos
eleven fifty for a gent's cut
smells of sun & smacks of
American Crew pomade
while the orange perma-
tannèd ones slather
factor fifteen all along
the promenade
just elegant enough to
roast

                I think
the halite air, even the dust
born of astral collisions
is rooted in the sand
of tidal demarcations

& the short-short-wearers
chic shore-dwellers
under an elongated sun-path
have sweat in the estuary's
mouth since time immemorial

                Solid as sun-eyed K'inich
                Ahau welling up saltwater
                awaiting solar transformation
                in this aquatic
                east paradise   now

                his metallic aviators
                irradiate.

Banks

Slow, cold tide.
The waterline's low
and every thing below it
falls out of the world.
Perhaps it is time
were we not allowed our secrets
to find and pull them from
the Earth's wet basement.
But I would not go looking
for nearly so long
under that mud-shelf and the
split, dry rushes. They, too,
struggle with their dignity
when stripped to the air's weight
and high, clean sight.

Molly Shrimpton
A Relationship with Rock

I am not a good climber. In fact, for a long time I was distinctly unwilling to lift even a tentative toe from the stability of the ground. Preferring the freedom of hiking, striding easily over hills, up mountains and across open country, I found myself thwarted, frustrated and perplexed in front of an imposing rock face, the views and panoramas it obscured limited to those who could scale its heights. I could not understand why my partner was so determined that I should undertake, and even enjoy this pursuit. But over time I have learnt to enjoy it, and to be enthusiastic about the abilities it has afforded me, and the places that it takes me. I have learnt to appreciate the access to those secret and magical locations that can only be gained by the ancient dialogue of hands, feet and rock.

My memories of climbing now echo across a broad mosaic of beautiful places. I have stood amongst hundreds of neon-clad others at the famous gritstone crags of the Peak district. I have breathed deeply the warm, salty breeze that strokes the white cliffs of Portland. I have struggled against the splintering, chaffing schist of New Zealand's Southern Alps, as well as the notoriously sloping limestone crags that rise alongside the cool waters of Payne's Ford. I have been caught short up a multi-pitch gone very wrong in the crags of Northland, anxiously watching a storm breast the skies towards us over the towering Kauri trees. I have had the breath torn from my throat whilst looking down the thundering Yosemite Valley from a modest ways up one of its iconic granite faces. I have been grated, grazed and sliced by the murderous stone of the Joshua Tree Desert's bizarre boulder piles, watched by the equally bizarre frozen forms of the Joshua trees themselves. I have sweated and sworn in the searingly hot gulleys and dusty folds of Arizona's astonishing Red Rocks canyon. And I have found wonder on the spectacular rock formations of Lone Pine, with the Sierra Nevada soaring on the horizon in one direction, and the dark lowlands of Death Valley stretching out in the other.

Each experience has provided insight into the strange world of climbers. I have learnt about the different types of rock, and the different ways of engaging with them, all unique in ways only my fingers and palms can attest to. Slowly I have stopped feeling like an alien. I have learnt a new language, understanding the use of each of the many different pieces of equipment: slings, nuts, cams, karabiners, belay plates, gri-gris and tat, as well as adding to my repertoire phrases of the climbing vernacular, such as 'beta', 'bomber', 'run out', 'pumpy', 'crimpy' and 'on-sight'. I have come to understand the rationale behind buying climbing shoes that are intentionally five sizes too small, and to expect and sympathize with the wails and groans of the wearer. I have gained an appreciation of what rock climbing can offer: pain, laughter, fury, joy, and wonder. As well as this, my muscles have strengthened, my fear subsided, and I have learnt to trust and to know my body. It has also become very apparent to me that climbing in a gym and climbing on a rock face are two completely different pursuits. Unlike indoor climbing - where every hold is highlighted in neon paint and virtually every move mapped out and dictated to you - outdoor climbing requires problem solving, and provides an opportunity to explore the ways in which our minds work. Faced with the obstacle of verticality, climbers must tune their brain to the minute detail of the rock's character, examining it for potential holds, analyzing it for patterns, and devising new sequences of order from its apparent chaos. Climbing has also given me a wider, more important understanding of the ways in which I experience and participate in place and environment. Each rock face, cliff and crag gives voice to the enormity of geological time; the stone is inscribed with the stories of its existence. I have spoken to many climbers, and among them have noted a recurrent appreciation for being in touch with something beyond the human, for reaching a mental state achieved only through vital contact and physical closeness to something far larger and more immense than we can know. To climb is to communicate with the bones of the Earth. To journey up the reaches of rock is to read one of its many histories, and to begin to know a version of its primal story. Of course, climbers do not pretend to be geologists or archaeologists, but they have an appreciation for the diversities of rock, and the subtleties of its different architectures, that many are not afforded. Climbing is a sport, but rather than providing contest between humans, it offers the opportunity to measure oneself against the immensity of the Earth.

I recently climbed at Chepstow. Perched on the border between England and Wales, it is a mecca of quarried limestone cliffs, which tower above the brown, muddied waters of the River Wye. It was early April, and a pair of peregrines had chosen an adjacent cliff for their nest. My powers of attention were tested when they flew overhead, one of them carrying the lumpen body of a pigeon. Lifeless in the quenching talons, its size attested to the formidable power of the falcon. After feeding, the pair circled above us, gliding on silken thermals, agitated by crows they swooped and swerved, curled round and soared across the cloudless sky. Small and inconsequential, I clung on to the cliff far below, squinting up, blinded by the sun and the heat radiating off the rock, yet unable to tear my gaze away from the luminous sky.

Climbing has put me in contact with my surroundings in a very different way. It has taken me to places that I never thought possible, and along the way it has taught me to wonder about what is beyond. It has outlined to me the limits of my strength, and the vulnerability of my body in the natural world, and in parallel has encouraged me to recognize the boundaries and borders of my understanding. Some consider climbing and mountaineering forms of conquest, they see recreation as mastery; they climb to claim. For me, these pursuits offer an opportunity to remind ourselves that the world is much more than the humans within it; more in fact, than we as a species will ever know. Climbing is an opportunity for exploration: of the world, of the self, and of the self in the world. Regardless of where I am, I never feel more mortal than when struggling up a rock face, and never smaller than when at the top.

About the Contributors

Ruth Bradshaw spent most of her career in a range of policy and research roles in the public sector, and now works for an environmental charity and studies MA Wild Writing at the University of Essex. Childhood holidays in Snowdonia left her with a life-long love of mountains, and she still likes to spend as much time as possible outdoors - walking, cycling or conservation volunteering.

Barbara Claridge is undertaking the Wild Writing MA at the University of Essex as a full-time student. Following a long career as head teacher of a Hampshire junior school, where outdoor learning was a passion, she moved to Brittany with her husband and began a five-year renovation/construction project of a longère and garden. She has also worked with the British Council in Beijing and Pittsburgh on the International Headteacher Programme and completed short-term voluntary work as a Primary Education Adviser in Ghana and Namibia. She tweets @56190bjc.

Wendy Constance had a career in textile design before she started writing stories squeezed between freelance work and single parenting. Winner of the Times/Chicken House Children's Fiction Competition 2013, her Stone Age adventure *Brave* was published April 2014. After 34 years in Yorkshire she moved back to Essex in 2010. She works part-time at Essex University as a notetaker. Wendy is studying MA Wild Writing, which combines her love of writing, nature, and walking, with the potential to interweave different creative practices.

Steph Driver has worked in the education, electricity, health and community sectors. She has debated in ecumenical, secular and interfaith groups, camped and hiked, cycled, bungee jumped, and (briefly) flown an aeroplane. She takes photographs and notes, and calculates, imagines, writes, draws, programs and knits. She talks a lot, and endeavours to listen. Sometimes she succeeds. She is currently undertaking a PhD at the University of Essex.

Simon Everett is a poet completing his PhD in Creative Writing at the University of Essex, funded by the ARHC (CHASE). His poetry has been anthologised in various places, and his translations have appeared in poetry magazines such as STAND. He most recently translated the poetry of the Chinese poet Zhang Yangyang for the Chinese Arts and Letters journal. His translations of Yu Xuanji previously featured in Creel 2. He is experimenting with computer aided constrained writing and text in unprintable media.

Elaine Ewart is working towards a PhD in Creative Writing at the University of Essex. In 2016, her play *In the Wake of the Flood* was commissioned for the Peterborough Green Festival and produced by the Eastern Angles theatre company. In 2015 she won second prize in the New Welsh Writing Awards and was shortlisted for the Resurgence Ecopoetry Awards. Elaine held the post of Fenland Poet Laureate in 2012, and continues to host poetry events and workshops in Cambridgeshire. Her work has been published in various journals and anthologies, including Creel 2. She also blogs for Flight Feather.

Jonathan King is currently studying MA Creative Writing at Essex University and is a member of Colchester Write Night, a Colchester based writing group who meet monthly at 15 Queen Street. Occasionally he can be heard reading his words at various locations.

Emma Kittle-Pey is a short fiction writer, currently working on her PhD at the University of Essex. She previously studied the MA in Creative Writing, and her first degree was in Politics with Economics from the University of Bath. She is founder and host of Colchester Write Night. Her second collection of short fiction, Gold Adornments, was published by Patrician Press in March 2017. It draws on her unique observations of home, work and life, always with something bigger in mind – her characters' survival in the current political and economic climate.

Melissa Shales is a part-time PhD Creative Writing student, travel writer, and teacher. Brought up in Zimbabwe, her first degree was in History and Archaeology. Her previous work includes writing over 30 guidebooks, series editing for the AA, Thomas Cook and Insight Guides. She is currently working on a narrative travel book exploring the history and social impact of the railways between Cairo and Cape Town. Melissa is a Winston Churchill Fellow, a Fellow of the Royal Geographical Society, and an Honorary Life Member of the British Guild of Travel Writers.

Judith Wolton is a retired teacher and a student on the MA Wild Writing Course. She has always been interested in poetry, particularly about edgelands and saltmarshes, and introduces it into her coursework. Various poems have been placed in local competitions, and some have been published in a variety of anthologies and magazines. She is a member of Mosaic Poetry Stanza, Colchester, and a regular attender at poetryWivenhoe. She has co-edited two anthologies of poetry with Pam Job of poetryWivenhoe: *So too have the doves gone*, and *Ornith-ology*. She runs a small creative writing group in Brooklands, Jaywick.

About the Editors

Danielle Bell is an MA Creative Writing student at University of Essex, having graduated from UCP Marjon in 2013 with a BA (Hons) Creative Writing. She is currently researching and creating a dissertation about 'Saying the Unsayable' – exploring topics surrounding trauma that people do not or cannot talk about, and trying to find ways to express these artistically. She was the winner of the 'Best Presentation of Dissertation topic' at the 2017 MA Conference for the LiFTs department, and used the prize money to buy more books to pile onto her collection of overflowing bookshelves. Although she is also expecting her first child this year, she hopes to complete her thesis soon and progress to starting a PhD, specialising in writing fictionally about complex and challenging themes.

Lelia Ferro is an MA Creative Writing student at the University of Essex. She also has an MA in Multimedia Journalism and a Postgraduate Diploma in Psychodynamic Approaches. Lelia spent nearly 20 years working in the media in London, before deciding to focus on her creative writing. She mainly writes poetry about hidden voices in the Essex landscape. She has lived in Wivenhoe for 10 years, and has had several poems published in *Words Down the Line*, a free leaflet available at Wivenhoe railway station. In 2017 she won the Bang Said The Gun open mic competition at Colchester Arts Centre with her poem about goths in the 90s.

Molly Shrimpton is a postgraduate student at the University of Essex, currently studying the MA Wild Writing: Literature, Landscape and Environment. She has a BA from the University of Kent in English and American Literature. She is currently working as an editor for the University academic journal ESTRO. Her main interests lie in Ecocriticsm, Animal Studies and the work of Virginia Woolf. She is currently writing her dissertation, which explores concepts of wilderness in contemporary travel narratives.

Marieke Sjerps is a third year Creative Writing PhD student at the University of Essex. Her research interests include existential philosophy, mythology, science fiction, and chivalric romance. The fictional component of her thesis will consist of a science fiction novel, titled *The Leap*, which imaginatively transforms the works of Socrates, Kierkegaard and Nietzsche. The critical commentary will examine the relationship between the witnessing of an aesthetic transformation and the possibility of a corresponding change in one's ethical identity. She is currently working as a graduate teaching assistant on The Enlightenment in the Centre of Interdisciplinary Studies at the University of Essex.

Acknowledgements

The Editorial Team would like to thank the following people for their assistance in helping to produce Creel3:

Sue Finn
Wivenhoe Bookshop

Phil Terry
Director of the Centre for Creative Writing
Departmental Head at LiFTS

The LiFTS Administration Team